PENGUIN CLASSICS

THE DOUBLE DEATH OF QUINCAS WATER-BRAY

JORGE AMADO (1912–2001), the son of a cocoa planter, was born in the Brazilian state of Bahia, which he would portray in more than thirty novels. His first novels, published when he was still a teenager, dramatize the class struggles of workers on Bahian cocoa plantations. Amado was later exiled for his leftist politics, but his novels would always have a strong political perspective. Not until Amado returned to Brazil in the 1950s did he write his acclaimed novels *Gabriela, Clove and Cinnamon* and *Dona Flor and Her Two Husbands* (the basis for the successful film and Broadway musical of the same name), which display a lighter, more comic approach than his overtly political novels. One of the most renowned writers of the Latin American boom of the 1960s, Amado has had his work translated into more than forty-five languages.

GREGORY RABASSA is a National Book Award–winning translator whose English-language versions of works by Gabriel García Márquez, Mario Vargas Llosa, Julio Cortázar, and Jorge Amado have become classics in their own right. He was born in Yonkers, New York, in 1922, and in 2006 he was awarded the National Medal of Arts. He is Professor Emeritus of Romance Languages and Comparative Literature at Queens College, City University of New York.

RIVKA GALCHEN is one of *The New Yorker*'s "20 Under 40" fiction writers and the author of the award-winning novel *Atmospheric Disturbances*. Her essays and stories have appeared in *Harper's Magazine, The New Yorker, Bookforum,* and *The New York Times*.

T0200828

JORGE AMADO

The Double Death of Quincas Water-Bray

Translated by
GREGORY RABASSA

Introduction by
RIVKA GALCHEN

PENGUIN BOOKS

PENGUIN BOOKS
Published by the Penguin Group
Penguin Group (USA) Inc., 375 Hudson Street, New York, New York 10014, U.S.A.
Penguin Group (Canada), 90 Eglinton Avenue East, Suite 700, Toronto, Ontario, Canada M4P 2Y3
(a division of Pearson Penguin Canada Inc.)
Penguin Books Ltd, 80 Strand, London WC2R 0RL, England
Penguin Ireland, 25 St Stephen's Green, Dublin 2, Ireland (a division of Penguin Books Ltd)
Penguin Group (Australia), 250 Camberwell Road, Camberwell,
Victoria 3124, Australia (a division of Pearson Australia Group Pty Ltd)
Penguin Books India Pvt Ltd, 11 Community Centre, Panchsheel Park, New Delhi – 110 017, India
Penguin Group (NZ), 67 Apollo Drive, Rosedale, Auckland 0632, New Zealand
(a division of Pearson New Zealand Ltd)
Penguin Books (South Africa) (Pty) Ltd, 24 Sturdee Avenue, Rosebank,
Johannesburg 2196, South Africa

Penguin Books Ltd, Registered Offices:
80 Strand, London WC2R 0RL, England

This translation first published in Penguin Books 2012

1   3   5   7   9   10   8   6   4   2

Published in Portuguese under the title *A morte e a morte de Quincas Berro Dagua* by Livraria
Martins Editora, Sao Paulo, 1961.

Publisher's Note
This is a work of fiction. Names, characters, places, and incidents either are the product of the
author's imagination or are used fictitiously, and any resemblance to actual persons, living or
dead, business establishments, events, or locales is entirely coincidental.

LIBRARY OF CONGRESS CATALOGING IN PUBLICATION DATA
Amado, Jorge, 1912–2001.
[Morte e a morte de Quincas Berro Dágua. English]
The double death of Quincas Water-Bray / Jorge Amado ; translated from the Portuguese by
Gregory Rabassa ; introduction by Rivka Galchen.
p. cm.—(Penguin classics)
ISBN 978-0-14-310636-4 (pbk.)
I. Rabassa, Gregory. II. Title.
PQ9697.A647M613 2012
869.3'41—dc23   2012022838

Printed in the United States of America
Set in Sabon

Contents

Introduction

Though a best seller in Brazil, and translated into more languages than most Americans know exist, the twentieth-century Brazilian writer Jorge Amado (1912–2001) is little known in this country, even to the bookish, for whom the writing of Brazil is represented either by the two genius Europhilic stars, Machado de Assis and Clarice Lispector—who, to be fair in the distribution of unfairness, are also relatively unknown in this country—or by the self-help-esque novelist/guru/lyricist Paulo Coelho, who is well known most everywhere, and who is not infrequently photographed with halo lighting effects, or barefoot in desert sand. So an American reader, educated in only these two extreme types, tends to feel at a loss even in building a misleading stereotype from which to begin misimagining what type of writer Amado might be. But maybe the Hydratic stereotype is a helpful beginning. Amado's work is neither precisely for the mandarin nor precisely for the masses. Amado held the prestigious chair of the Brazilian Academy of Letters for forty years, and he was especially beloved by his contemporary French intellectuals; at the same time, his novels sold so well, and there were so many of them (more than thirty), that these days—from our place and time—one might understandably entertain the incorrect suspicion that Amado had penned series with zombies, or with vampires, or both.

In fact, Amado wrote mostly about the lives of the people—most of them quite poor—from his native region of Bahia, Brazil. Yet, the varieties of the undead prove to be a not fruitless misassociation to bring to a first reading of this 1959 novella, *The Double Death of Quincas Water-Bray*, published here in celebration of the centennial of Amado's birth. A swift, funny, and occasionally even slapstick little book, *Double Death* is not uninterested in clouding a reader's sense of in what ways and when its eponymic hero is and isn't alive, and in what ways and when he was and wasn't, at certain moments, dead. (Normally I might worry such a sentence would plot-spoil, but one of the unsettling comforts of reading a Latin American novel—the "Latin American novel" being the taxonomical juggernaut with which every book penned south of Brownsville, Texas, has to contend, even those penned in Portuguese—is that a character's death rarely means that character then exits stage left forever; only in Shakespeare do the dead as frequently return.)

So who is this Quincas? In the novel's opening, Quincas is already dead. The reader really hears only rumors of him, and for a spell we are not even sure Quincas is his "real" name. We are told that he was born Joaquim Soares da Cunha, "of good family; and exemplary employee of the State Bureau of Revenue, with a measured step, a closely shaved chin, a black alpaca jacket, and a briefcase under his arm; someone listened to with respect by his neighbors as he rendered his opinions on politics and the weather, never seen in any bar, with a modest drink of cachaça at home." This seems to be the story his family tries to maintain and spread. "When a man dies he is reintegrated into his most authentic respectability, even having committed the maddest acts when he was alive. . . . This was the thesis put forth by the family and seconded by neighbors and friends."

But there are other theses. Arguably the really important cast of characters in *Double Death* consists not of people but rather of gossip, rumor, hearsay, stories, and lies—how they are born, countered, stamped dubiously onto official papers, re-countered, wiped out, and reborn, and not just anywhere but very specifically in Quincas's (and Amado's) region of Bahia, Brazil.

Ten years before his death, Joaquim Soares unexpectedly called his wife and daughter "vipers" and then, "with the greatest of calm in the world, as if he were simply carrying through some exceedingly banal act, he left and never came back." He then took to drinking, gambling, prankstering, socializing with the lower classes, and, possibly, became much happier. He also became much more talked about.

For the family of Joaquim Soares, the rumor and hearsay about Quincas—they can hardly acknowledge it is the same person—are experienced as a humiliation, even a sort of assault. "'The king of the tramps of Bahia,' the police news column in the newspapers had written about him, a street type mentioned in the chronicles by literary people . . ." Quincas's son-in-law, Leonardo, recalls with particular shame and disgust a day when he found his father-in-law at a police station "in the basement of headquarters, barefoot and in his undershorts, gambling peacefully with thieves and swindlers." The word on the street, or one of the words, was that Quincas Water-Bray—a nickname he earned, we hear, when after having taken a drink of water he had thought was cachaça, he then spat it out and shouted about as if he'd just swallowed poison—felt his respectable life was a living death; that in leaving it, he became his free and natural and joyful self.

When an image vendor—an image vendor! one "who had a shop on the Ladeira do Tabuão"—brings the news of

Quincas's being found dead alone in his room, Quincas's estranged daughter and son-in-law sigh in relief. No more humiliating rumors, they think. But of course there are more. "The rascals who told the story of Quincas's final moments up and down the streets in the hillside neighborhoods, across from the market and in the stalls at Água dos Meninos (there was even a handbill with some doggerel composed by the improviser Cuíca de Santo Amaro that was widely sold), were therefore an affront to the memory of the deceased, according to his family." The novel is a battle of spin. "These would be difficult moments for Leonardo, talking about the old man's madness, trying to find some explanation for it. The worst of it would be the news spreading among his colleagues, whispered from desk to desk as faces took on wicked little smiles, uncouth tales were told, tasteless comments made."

The presence of so many commentaries and columns draws extra attention to the question: Who or what, then, is the novella's voice outside of quotes? The voice is not unrelated to the opening of *Pride and Prejudice*, not unrelated to the townspeak of *Chronicle of a Death Foretold*, not unrelated to what it might sound like if the speakers in *As I Lay Dying* were allowed out of the corrals of their separate chapters so they could shoulder up against one another within the same sentence. The voice is a fractious and fractionating family of voices figuring out something about how the stories we tell contribute to the construction of the lives we live and the deaths we die. The voice is also, if sides are to be taken, in alliance with Quincas's friends more than Joaquim's family—the name Quincas is used more often, and the telling itself is an act of solidarity.

For while gossip and rumor register like mortal wounds to the family, Quincas and his buddies are of the variety such that the only thing worse than being talked about is not being talked about. Hence, Quincas's family's aggression is to not speak of him. "It had reached the point where his name was never mentioned or his deeds ever spoken about in the innocent presence of the children, for whom Grandfather Joaquim, of fond memory, had died a long time ago, decently enwrapped in everybody's respect." And his friends' retaliation is to speak and speak.

The family tries to have a decent wake for Joaquim. They buy him some nice, but not too pricey, new clothes—and even some shoes, which they can barely afford. (They pass on buying him new underwear, since they feel it can respectfully be done without.) And they try to make sure no one will know he's dead until it's too late to visit the body, until the wake is over. But the family gets tired, keeping vigil with the body, and when Quincas's friends come by to pay their respects—they hear about the wake because Bahia is a place where one hears about things—the family retires to rest. Quincas's friends gossip. They drink. They tell stories of their friend. They even steal his shoes. They offer their dead friend something to drink as well, so that he can be included in the fun. And then their friend—or at least the story goes—comes back to life for one more good night on the town, one more visit to his mistress, and one final death, one of his own choosing: leaping into the sea and disappearing without a trace.

Quincas, who is more than once in the novel termed a champion of dying—he dies not once, not twice, but three times!—is in this way also a champion of being born, at least via story. As such, it is fitting that gossip prompts Quincas back to life, at least long enough to see to his own funeral. "Gossip," if we allow ourselves to follow the word's roots in English, derives from *gossib*, Middle English for a woman invited to be present at a birth. Invited women were meant to chatter idly, to amuse and distract the laboring mother from pain and boredom. (At least "gossip" most likely derives from *gossib*—etymologies are rumors as well.)

Of Bahia, the region of Brazil where most of Amado's work is set, the wider world heard rumor in Claude Lévi-Strauss's *Tristes Tropiques*. In the opening section, after Lévi-Strauss speaks dismissively of the whole genre of tales of travel, and shortly before he notes that he never, at the time, knew what he was searching out, he describes a brief port-of-call visit to Bahia, a little before the outbreak of World War II. He recalls going from church to church—"there are said to be 365 of them," he notes, "one for each day of the year they say"—photographing architectural details. While doing so, a group of "half-naked" black boys are following him, begging him not for money but simply to also be photographed. He is charmed and eventually agrees. "I had barely gone two hundred yards further when a hand descended on my shoulder: two plain-clothes inspectors . . . informed me that I had just committed an unfriendly act towards Brazil: the photograph, if used in Europe, might possibly give credence to the legend that there were black-skinned Brazilians and that the urchins of Bahia went barefoot."

Lévi-Strauss's trip follows shortly after the release of Amado's sixth novel, *Captains of the Sands* (1937), the story of a band of boys living in a shack near the sea and making their way through petty crimes in Bahia. Amado was not yet thirty at the time. His work had already been banned, he had been imprisoned for two months on charges of being involved in a communist conspiracy, and he was about to be imprisoned a second time. His 1935 novel, *Jubiabá*, follows the life of a poor black slum boy who eventually becomes a dockworker and labor organizer; his 1936 novel, *Sea of Death*, follows the life of Bahia sailors. *The Knight of Hope*, published in 1941, was about an abolitionist poet from

Bahia's past; after that, Amado was in exile in Argentina and Uruguay for a couple years. He later served the Brazilian Communist Party as their representative in the National Constituent Assembly, then lived in France and Czechoslovakia for a number of years. In 1951 he accepted the Stalin Peace Prize; in 1955 he returned to Brazil; in 1956, after Khrushchev's denunciation of Stalin, he left the Communist Party. He had decided to leave political life and devote himself exclusively to literature. He began writing more books from the point of view of women. He wrote more often, and very frankly, about sex. (Perhaps not coincidentally, his writing also became more humorous.) For a time, his work was considered so racy and such an offense to morals that he was not welcome in his own hometown of Ilhéus. Amado's 1966 bedroom comic novel, *Dona Flor and Her Two Husbands*—a woman is haunted by the disapproving ghost of her dead husband when she takes up a new and less sexually interesting lover—became a best seller, and eventually a hit Brazilian film starring Sônia Braga, and then a sanitized American rom-com with Sally Field. Amado wrote more novels, wrote some children's stories; many more films were made of his work—also TV series, cartoons, ballets, even Samba routines. . . .

In Bahia today, Amado's house stands as a museum and foundation; it is one of the main sites to which local luxury hotels demarcate their nearness. Which, one imagines, must feel funny to a man who consistently went to such pains to list the price of the garments purchased—and the underwear not purchased—for a corpse, and whose work was serially revered, reviled, revered again, reviled again, and on and on, most precisely for his interest in writing lovingly and in economic detail about the lives of the lower classes. More than one expert of sorts on Latin American literature described Amado to me as something akin to great but somewhat dismissable as a sentimental Marxist. *The Double Death of Quincas Water-Bray* recounts the stories told about a dead man; with some irony we note the biography of Jorge Amado today as just more stories about the dead man in the room with us. It seems time to restore some life to him by starting newer, more interesting, and perhaps more true rumors about this sui generis novelist.

RIVKA GALCHEN

For Zélia, by the fish-skiff docks

For the memory of Carlos Pena Filho,
Master of poetry and life, A little Water-Bray
at a tavern table, thin and pale-faced lord of
the poker game, sailing today on an unknown sea
with his angel wings, This tale here that I told
him once I'd tell.

For Laís and Rui Antunes, in whose fraternal
Pernambuco house with warmth of friendship Quincas
and his people came to be.

Let everyone see to his own funeral; nothing is impossible.
—The last words of Quincas Water-Bray,
according to Quitéria, who was at his side

The Double Death of
Quincas Water-Bray

I

Even today a certain confusion remains surrounding the death of Quincas Water-Bray. Doubts to be explained, absurd details, contradictions in the testimony of witnesses, diverse gaps. Nothing is clear as to time, place, and last words. The family, backed up by neighbors and friends, remains adamant with their version of a peaceful death in the morning, without witnesses, display, or last words, taking place almost twenty hours before that other demise, the one bandied about and commented upon as the night wanes and the moon disappears over the sea, when mysteries take place along the waterfront of Bahia. Spoken in the presence of competent witnesses, however, and talked about everywhere in hillside neighborhoods and hidden alleys, his last words are repeated from mouth to mouth and in the opinion of those people represent more than just a farewell to the world; they are a prophetic testimony, a message with deep meaning (as a young author of our own time would come to write).

All those competent witnesses, among them Master Manuel and Quitéria Goggle-Eye, a woman of her word, and yet, in spite of it all, there are those who deny all and any authenticity, not to those admired words alone but also to all the events of that memorable night when at a doubtful time and under disputable circumstances Quincas

Water-Bray plunged into the seas of Bahia and set off on an endless journey, never to return. That's what the world's like, hitched, like oxen to a yoke, to law and order, customary procedures, and sealed documents. They triumphantly display the death certificate, signed by the doctor just before noon, and on the strength of that simple sheet of paper—just because it has printed letters and some stamps on it—they try to snuff out all those hours lived so intensely by Quincas Water-Bray up until his departure, of his own free and spontaneous will, as he declared in a loud, clear voice to his friends and all present.

The dead man's family—his respectable daughter and his proper son-in-law, a civil servant with a promising career; Aunt Marocas; and his younger brother, a merchant with modest credit in the bank—says that the whole tale is nothing but a gross bit of counterfeit goods, the inventions of inveterate drunkards and lowlifes on the margin of society and the law, rogues whose surroundings ought to be the bars of a jail cell and not the freedom of the streets, the waterfront of Bahia, its white sand beaches and its immense night. Committing an injustice, it is to these friends of Quincas that they attribute all the responsibility for the ill-fated existence he had been living these last few years, when he became a bother and a shame for his family. It had reached the point where his name was never mentioned or his deeds ever spoken about in the innocent presence of the children, for whom Grandfather Joaquim, of fond memory, had died a long time ago, decently enwrapped in everybody's respect. Which leads one to attest that there had indeed been a first death, if not physical, a moral one at least, dating back some years earlier, which brings the total to three, making Quincas some kind of record holder in matters of death, a champion at dying, and gives us the right to think that posterior events—beginning with the death certificate right up to his plunge into the sea—were a farce he put together in order to molest his relatives' lives once more, to bring some annoyance into their existence, lowering them into the shameful gossip of the street. He wasn't a man for respect and convention, in spite of the respect he was paid by his card-playing partners as a gambler of outsized luck or as a drinker of storied amounts of cachaça.

I don't know if this mystery of the death (of the successive deaths) of Quincas Water-Bray will ever be completely deciphered, but I shall make an attempt, as he himself advised, because the important thing is to try, even with the impossible.

2

The rascals who told the story of Quincas's final moments up and down the streets in the hillside neighborhoods, across from the market and in the stalls at Água dos Meninos (there was even a handbill with some doggerel composed by the improviser Cuíca de Santo Amaro that was widely sold), were therefore an affront to the memory of the deceased, according to his family. And the memory of the dead, as is well known, is a sacred thing, not meant for the unclean mouths of cachaça-swillers, gamblers, and marijuana smugglers. Nor to serve as the basis for the vulgar poetry of the singers of popular songs by the entrance to the Lacerda Elevator, which so many proper people pass through, including the colleagues of Leonardo Barreto, Quincas's humiliated son-in-law. When a man dies he is reintegrated into his most authentic respectability, even having committed the maddest acts when he was alive. Death, with its unseen hand, erases the stains of the past and leaves the dead man's memory gleaming like a new-cut diamond. This was the thesis put forth by the family and seconded by neighbors and friends. According to them, Quincas Water-Bray, upon dying, went back to being that once respectable Joaquim Soares da Cunha, of good family; an exemplary employee of the State Bureau of Revenue, with a measured step, a closely shaved chin, a black alpaca jacket, and a briefcase under his arm;

someone listened to with respect by his neighbors as he rendered his opinions on politics and the weather, never seen in any bar, with only a modest drink of cachaça at home. In reality, in an effort worthy of applause, the family had managed to arrange for Quincas's memory to gleam forth without a flaw only a few years after having publicly declared him to be dead. They spoke of him in the past tense when circumstances obliged them to make mention of him. Unfortunately, however, every so often some neighbor, some colleague of Leonardo's, a talkative friend of Vanda's (his shamed daughter) would run into Quincas or hear something about him from some third party. It was as if a dead man had risen from his tomb to cast a stain on his own memory: lying drunk in the sun at the height of morning near the Rampa do Mercado, or, filthy and ragged, leaning against some greasy cart by the steps of the church of Pilar, or even singing in a hoarse voice on the arms of black and mulatto streetwalkers along the Ladeira de São Miguel. A horror!

When finally on that morning a vendor of holy images who had a shop on the Ladeira do Tabuão arrived in great affliction at the small but well-kept home of the Barreto family and brought the daughter, Vanda, and the son-in-law, Leonardo, the news that Quincas had indeed kicked the bucket, found dead in his miserable hovel, a sigh of relief arose in unison from the breasts of the couple. From now on it would no longer be the memory of the retired employee of the State Bureau of Revenue overturned and dragged through the mud by the contradictory acts of the tramp he had been transformed into toward the end of his life. The time for a bit of deserved rest had arrived. Now they could speak freely of Joaquim Soares da Cunha; praise his conduct as a civil servant, a husband and father, a citizen; point out his virtues as an example for the children; teach them to love the memory of their grandfather without fear of any upset.

The image vendor, a skinny old man with close-curled white hair, went into details: A black woman who sold *mingau*, *acarajé*, *abará*, and other culinary delights had had some important business to transact with Quincas that morning. He had promised to get her some herbs that were hard to find but that were indispensable for the obligations of *candomblé* rites. The black woman had come for the herbs. It was urgent that she get them because it was the holy season for festivities in honor of Xangô. As usual, the door to the room at the top of the filthy stairway was open—Quincas had lost the great and ancient key a long time ago. It was said that he'd sold it to some tourists on a day that was lean from his bad luck in gambling, as he coupled it to a tale, with dates and all, that elevated it to the status of a holy key to a church. The woman called out but got no answer. She thought he was asleep and pushed open the unlocked door. Quincas was there smiling as he lay on his cot—the sheet was black with filth, and a ragged blanket covered his legs—but it was his usual smile of welcome, so she thought nothing of it. She asked him for the herbs he'd promised her, but he smiled without answering. The great toe of his right foot stuck out through a hole in the sock, and his beat-up shoes were on the floor. The black woman, a close friend and quite accustomed to Quincas's monkeyshines, sat down on the bed and told him to get a move on. She was surprised he hadn't reached out a libertine hand, addicted as he was to pats and pinches. She stared again at the great toe of his right foot, found it strange. She touched Quincas's body and jumped up in alarm, dropping the cold hand. She ran down the stairs and spread the news.

It was with scant pleasure that the daughter and

son-in-law listened to those details about the black woman
and the herbs, the gropings, and the *candomblé*. They nodded their heads as they hurried the image vendor along. He
was a calm man, and he liked to tell a story in full. He was
the only one who knew about Quincas's relatives, revealed
to him once during a night of heavy drinking, and that was
why he'd come. He put on a remorseful face and proffered
his heartfelt condolences.

It was time for Leonardo to leave for the office, so he told
his wife, "You go on ahead over there. I'll stop by the office
and won't be long in joining you. I've got to sign in. I'll talk
to the boss."

They invited in the image vendor and offered him a chair
in the living room. Vanda went to change her clothes. The
vendor was talking to Leonardo about Quincas. There was
nobody on the Ladeira do Tabuão who didn't like him. Why
did he take up that life of a tramp, a man from a good family and property, as the vendor could see after having the
pleasure of getting to know his daughter and son-in-law?
Some kind of trouble? It must have been. Maybe his wife
had been two-timing him; that happens a lot—and the vendor put his forefingers to his head in an imitation of horns,
his way of asking a lewd kind of question: Had he guessed
right?

"Dona Otacília, my mother-in-law, was a saint of a
woman!"

The vendor scratched his chin: Why then? But Leonardo
didn't answer. He went to take care of Vanda, who was
calling him from the bedroom.

"We've got to notify—"

"Notify? Who? Why?"

"Aunt Marocas and Uncle Eduardo . . . the neighbors.
Send out invitations to the funeral . . ."

"Why do we have to let the neighbors know now? We'll tell them later. If not, there'll be a damned lot of talk."

"But Aunt Marocas . . ."

"I'll talk to her and Eduardo . . . after I stop by the office. Hurry up or else this guy who came with the news will go spreading it all over town."

"Who could have thought? Dying like that, with nobody—"

"Whose fault is it? His own, the damned nut."

In the living room the image vendor was admiring a color photo of Quincas. It was an old one, from some fifteen years before. A dignified gentleman in a stiff collar, with a black tie, a mustache with pointed tips, shiny hair, and ruddy cheeks. Next to it, in an identical frame, with an accusing look and hard mouth, was Dona Otacília, wearing a black lace dress. The vendor studied her sour face. *She doesn't have the look of someone who's been cheating on her husband. On the other hand, she must have been a tough bone to gnaw. . . . Sainted woman? I don't believe it.*

3

Only a few people from the neighborhood were there looking at the corpse when Vanda arrived. The image vendor
informed them in a soft voice, "This is his daughter. He had
a daughter, a son-in-law, a brother, and a sister. Distin-
guished people. His son-in-law is a civil servant. He lives in
Itapagipe in a fine home."

They drew back to let her through, waiting with curiosity
for her to fling herself onto the corpse, to embrace it and
cover herself with tears, perhaps even to sob. On the cot,
Quincas Water-Bray, in his old mended pants, his tattered
shirt, a grease-stained vest that was too large for him, was
smiling as though enjoying it all. Vanda stood there, motionless, looking at the unshaven face, the filthy hands, the great
toe coming through the hole in his sock. She had no tears
left to weep or sobs to fill the room. Both had been used up
in the early days of Quincas's madness, when she had made
repeated attempts to bring him back to the home he'd abandoned. Now all she could do was look, her cheeks blushing
with shame.

He didn't make a very presentable corpse: the body of a
tramp who'd just happened to die, with no decorum in his
death, no respect, lying there and cynically laughing at her,
at Leonardo certainly, at the rest of the family. A cadaver
for the morgue, to go off in the black police hearse and later

serve students at the medical school in their practice sessions, to be buried finally in a shallow grave with no cross or headstone. It was the corpse of Quincas Water-Bray, drunkard, scoffer, and gambler, with no family or home, no flowers or prayers. It wasn't Joaquim Soares da Cunha, a proper civil servant at the State Bureau of Revenue, retired after twenty-five years of good and loyal service; a model husband whom everybody tipped his hat to and whose hand everybody shook. How could a man at the age of fifty abandon his family, his home, the habits of a lifetime, his circle of friends, to wander the streets, get drunk in cheap bars, frequent houses of prostitution, go about filthy and unshaven, live in a disgraceful hovel, sleep on a miserable cot? Vanda could find no valid explanation. Many times at night after the death of Dona Otacília—not even on that solemn occasion had Quincas deigned to return to the company of his people—she had discussed the matter with her husband. It wasn't insanity, at least not insanity of the asylum kind—the doctors were unanimous in that. How could it be explained, then?

But now all that had come to an end—that nightmare over the years, that stain on family dignity. Vanda had inherited a certain practical sense from her mother, a capacity for making quick decisions and carrying them out. As she stood staring at the dead man, that unpleasant caricature of what had once been her father, she was deciding what to do. First, call the doctor for the death certificate. Then, dress the body decently and have it carried to their home. Bury it beside Otacília after a not too expensive funeral (times were hard), one that wouldn't make them look bad in the eyes of friends, neighbors, or Leonardo's colleagues. Aunt Marocas and Uncle Eduardo would help. As she was pondering all this with her eyes fixed on Quincas's smiling face, Vanda wondered what was going to become of her father's pension. Would they inherit it, or would it just go back into the pension fund? Maybe Leonardo could find out. . . .

She turned toward the onlookers, who were staring at her. They were part of that rabble from Tabuão, the riffraff in whose company Quincas found pleasure. What were they doing there? Didn't they understand that Quincas Water-Bray had ceased to exist the moment he exhaled his last breath? That he had been nothing but an invention of the Devil? A bad dream? A nightmare? Joaquim Soares da Cunha would once again return to be among his people for a short time, in the comfort of a proper home, reinstalled in his respectability. The time for his return had arrived, and this time Quincas couldn't laugh in the face of his daughter and son-in-law, telling them to go peddle their potatoes, bidding them a sarcastic "bye-bye" and going off whistling. He was lying there on the cot, not moving. Quincas Water-Bray was all through.

Vanda lifted her head, took a victorious look at those present, and demanded, in that voice of Otacília's, "Is there something you want? If not, you can leave now." Then, speaking to the image vendor: "Would you please do me a favor and call a doctor? It's for the death certificate."

The vendor nodded. He was impressed. The others slowly left. Vanda was left alone with the corpse. Quincas Water-Bray was smiling, and the great toe of his right foot seemed to be growing larger in the hole in his sock.

4

She looked for a place to sit down. All there was beside the cot was an empty kerosene can. Vanda stood it up, blew the dust off, and sat down. How long was it going to take the doctor to get there? And what about Leonardo? She imagined her husband at the office, clumsily explaining to the boss the unexpected death of his father-in-law. Leonardo's boss had known Joaquim during his good days at the State Bureau of Revenue, so how could someone who'd known and respected him have imagined his end? These would be difficult moments for Leonardo, talking about the old man's madness, trying to find some explanation for it. The worst of it would be the news spreading among his colleagues, whispered from desk to desk as faces took on wicked little smiles, uncouth tales told, tasteless comments made. That father had been a cross to bear, making their lives a calvary, but now they had come to the top of the hill, and all that was needed was a little more patience. Vanda got a glimpse of the dead man out of the corner of her eye. There he was, smiling, finding all of that exceedingly amusing.

It's a sin to get angry at a dead man, especially so if he's your father. Vanda restrained herself. She was religious; she attended the Bonfim church. A bit of a spiritualist too, she believed in reincarnation. Besides, Quincas's smile didn't matter all that much now. She was in charge at last, and he would shortly go back to being the proper Joaquim Soares da Cunha, the irreproachable good citizen.

The image vendor returned with the doctor, a young fellow, obviously a recent graduate, as it was still hard for him to appear as a full and competent physician. The image vendor pointed to the dead man, and the doctor nodded to Vanda, opening his shiny new leather satchel. Vanda got up and moved the kerosene can away.

"What did he die of?"

It was the image vendor who explained: "They found him dead, just the way he is here."

"Was he ill?"

"I don't know. No, sir. I've known him for maybe ten years, and he was always healthy as an ox. Unless, doctor . . ."

"Yes?"

". . . you can call cachaça a sickness. He could toss off a good bit of it. He was pretty good at drinking."

Vanda coughed, concerned.

The doctor addressed her: "Did he work for you, ma'am?"

There was a brief, heavy silence. Her voice came from afar. "He was my father."

A young doctor, still inexperienced in life, he took measure of Vanda with his eyes, noted her proper attire, her neatness, her high heels. Then he looked back at the dead man and the indescribable poverty of that absolutely miserable room.

"Did he live here?"

"We did everything to get him to come home. He was . . ."

"Crazy?"

Vanda shrugged. She felt like crying. The doctor didn't

go on. He sat down on the edge of the bed and began his examination. He leaned his head over and said, "He's smiling, hah! The face of a jokester."

Vanda closed her eyes and clutched her hands, her face red with shame.

5

The family conference didn't last long. They discussed matters over the table of a restaurant in the Baixa dos Sapateiros. Along the busy streets the crowds were passing, happy and hurried. Right opposite was a movie theater. The corpse had been turned over to an undertaking establishment owned by a friend of Uncle Eduardo's. A 20 percent discount.

Uncle Eduardo was explaining, "What's really expensive is the coffin. And the cars, if there's a big turnout. A fortune. They won't even let you die today."

In a shop nearby they bought some new clothes (the material wasn't all that great, but, as Uncle Eduardo said, it was still too good to be eaten by worms): a pair of black shoes, a white shirt, a tie, and a pair of socks. There was no need for any underwear. Eduardo was jotting down every expense in a little notebook. He was master at cutting corners; his business prospered.

In the skillful hands of the specialists from the funeral parlor, Quincas Water-Bray was going back to being Joaquim Soares da Cunha while his relatives were eating fish stew in the restaurant and discussing the funeral arrangements. The only matter open to argument was one detail: Where would the coffin leave from?

Vanda had planned to bring the body home and hold the

wake in the living room, serving coffee and drinks for those present during the night. Calling Father Roque to bless the corpse. Holding the burial early in the morning so that a lot of people could come: colleagues from his office, old acquaintances, friends of the family. Leonardo was against it. Why bring the dead man home? Why invite friends and neighbors, inconveniencing a lot of people? So everyone could remember the wild things he had done in his unspeakable life of the last few years? To expose the family's shame to the whole world? That's how it had gone in his office that morning. They didn't talk about anything else. Every one of them knew some story about Quincas and would tell it with gales of laughter. He himself, Leonardo, had never imagined his father-in-law could have done so many and such wild things. Every one was enough to make your hair stand on end. . . . Not to mention that a lot of people thought Quincas was dead and buried or maybe living in the interior of the state. And what about the children? They had venerated the memory of an exemplary grandfather who was resting in God's holy peace, and all of a sudden their parents would be coming home carrying the corpse of a tramp, tossing him under the nose of the innocent children. And what about all the hard work they would have to do, and the mounting expenses of a funeral in addition to those of the burial and the new clothes, the new shoes. He, Leonardo, was in need of a pair of shoes. He'd sent out his very old pair to have half soles put on in order to save money. Now, with this splurge, how could he even be thinking about a new pair of shoes?

Aunt Marocas, a rather plump lady, in adoration of the fish stew they served in the restaurant, was of the same opinion. "The best thing would be to spread the word that he died in the interior, that we got a telegram. Then people could be invited to the seventh-day mass. Anyone who wants to can come, and we won't be obliged to provide transportation."

Vanda stopped eating. "In spite of all the trouble he's caused, he *is* my father. I don't want him to be buried like some tramp. If he were your father, would you like it, Leonardo?"

Uncle Eduardo wasn't all that sentimental. "So just what has he been, if not a tramp? And one of the worst in Bahia. Even though he's my brother, I can't deny that."

Aunt Marocas belched, her belly full, her heart too. "Poor Joaquim . . . He had a good nature. He never did anything out of meanness. He liked that life. Everyone has his own fate. He was like that ever since he was a child. Once—do you remember, Eduardo?—he tried to run off with a circus. He got a whipping that would have curled your hair." She patted Vanda, who was sitting next to her, on the thigh, as if to excuse herself. "And your mother, my dear, she *was* a bit bossy. So one day he just took off. He told me he wanted to be free, like a bird. He really was a funny man."

No one found it funny. Vanda tightened her face, went on with what she had been saying: "I'm not defending him. He put us through a lot, me and my mother, who was a fine woman. And Leonardo. But that's no reason for my wanting him to be buried like a stray dog. What would people say when they found out? Before he went crazy he was a respectable person. He should be buried in a proper way."

Leonardo looked at her with pleading eyes. He knew he wouldn't get anywhere arguing with Vanda. She always ended up imposing her opinion and her wishes. It had been that way too with Joaquim and Otacília, except that one day Joaquim chucked it all and took off. There was nothing else to do, then, but drag the body home and go about telling friends and acquaintances, inviting people by phone, spending the whole night awake listening to them tell tales about

Quincas, the muffled laughter, the winks, everything going on like that until they left for the cemetery. That father-in-law of his had made his life bitter, given the greatest of upsets. Leonardo had lived in apprehension of "another one of his stunts," of opening the newspaper and coming upon an item about his arrest for vagrancy, as had happened once. He didn't even want to remember that day when at Vanda's insistence he went to the police station and was sent from one place to another until he found Quincas in the basement of headquarters, barefoot and in his undershorts, gambling peacefully with thieves and swindlers. And after all that, now when he thought he could breathe easily, he still had to put up with that corpse for a whole day and night, and in his home. . . .

But Eduardo wasn't in favor either, and his opinion carried weight because the merchant had agreed to share the funeral expenses. "That's all very fine, Vanda. Let him be buried like a Christian, with a priest, new clothes, and a wreath. He doesn't deserve any of it, but he is your father and my brother after all. That's all very fine, but why have the body at home—?"

"Yeah, why?" Leonardo repeated like an echo.

". . . bothering a lot of people, having to rent six or seven limousines for the procession? Do you know how much each one costs? And carrying the body from Tabuão to Itapagipe? A fortune. Why can't the funeral start from right here? We'll make up the whole procession. All that will be needed is one car. Then, if you insist, you can send out invitations to the seventh-day mass."

"Tell them he died in the interior." Aunt Marocas hadn't abandoned her suggestion.

"Maybe so. Why not?"

"So who's going to sit up with the body?"

"Just us. Why should there be anyone else?"

Vanda ended up giving in. It was true, she thought. The idea of carting the body home was too much. It would only mean a lot of work, too much expense and bother. The best thing was to bury Quincas with the greatest discretion possible and then tell friends, invite them to the seventh-day mass. It was all set, then. They ordered dessert. A nearby loudspeaker was bellowing out the superiority of a real estate firm's sales plan.

6

Uncle Eduardo went back to his store. He couldn't leave it alone in the hands of his workers, a bunch of hoodlums. Aunt Marocas promised to come back later for the wake. She had to stop by her home; she'd left everything in a mess in the flurry of receiving the news. Leonardo, on the advice of Vanda herself, was taking the afternoon off from his office in order to visit the real estate company and complete the sale of a lot they were buying on an installment plan. One day, God willing, they would have their own house.

They had set up a kind of rotation, taking turns with the body: Vanda and Aunt Marocas in the afternoon, Leonardo and Uncle Eduardo at night. The Tabuão hillside neighborhood wasn't any place for a lady to be seen at night; it was a section with a bad reputation, filled with hooligans and ladies of the evening. The next morning the whole family would come together for the burial.

That was how Vanda found herself alone in the afternoon with her father's corpse. The sounds of a poor and intense life just reached the third floor of the tenement where the dead man was resting after the fatigue of having his clothes changed.

The men from the funeral parlor had done a good job. They were competent and well trained. The image vendor

had said when he stopped by for a moment to see how
things were going, "He doesn't even look dead." His hair
combed, shaved, dressed in black, a white shirt, and a tie,
with a pair of shined shoes, it really was Joaquim Soares da
Cunha who was resting in the coffin—a splendid casket
(Vanda stated this with satisfaction), with gold handles and
frills on the edges. They had improvised a kind of table with
some boards and sawhorses, and onto it they'd lifted the
noble and austere casket. Two large candles—the kind used
on a main altar, Vanda boasted—were giving off a weak
illumination because the light of Bahia was coming in
through the window and filling the room. All that sunshine,
so much merry light, seemed to Vanda to be a disrespect for
the dead as it negated the candles, taking away their august
light. For a moment she thought about snuffing them out,
for reasons of economy. But since the undertaker would no
doubt charge the same for the use of two or of ten candles,
she decided to shut the window, and shadows took over the
room as the holy flames leaped up again like tongues of fire.
Vanda sat down on a chair (a loan from the image vendor),
feeling satisfaction. Not the simple satisfaction of having
fulfilled her daughterly duty, but something deeper.

A complacent sigh escaped her breast. She fixed her
brown hair with her hands. It was as though she had finally
tamed Quincas, as though she were holding the reins again,
the ones he had torn from Otacília's strong hands one day
as he laughed in her face. The shadow of a smile bloomed
on Vanda's lips, and it might have been beautiful and desirable had not a certain firm hardness marked it. She felt
avenged for everything that Quincas had made the family
suffer, especially herself and Otacília. The humiliation of
all those years. There had been ten of them since Joaquim
had begun to lead that absurd life. "The king of the tramps
of Bahia," the crime blotter in the newspapers had said

about him, a street type mentioned in the chronicles by literary people, avid for something quick and picturesque.
Ten years of shame for the family as it was splashed with
the shame of that disreputable celebrity, the "boozer in
chief of Salvador," the "tatterdemalion philosopher of the
market dock," the "senator of honky-tonks," "Quincas
Water-Bray, tramp par excellence"—just look at the treatment he received from the newspapers, where they would
sometimes print a picture of him, all covered in filth. My
God: how much a daughter can suffer in this world where
fate has reserved for her the cross of a father with no aware-
ness at all of his duties.

But now she felt content, looking at the corpse in the
almost luxurious coffin, wearing a black suit, his hands
crossed over his chest in a pose of devout contrition. The
flames of the candles rose up, making his new shoes gleam.
Everything was quite proper, except for the room, of course.
It was a consolation for someone who had been so afflicted
and had suffered so much. Vanda felt that Otacília must be
feeling happy in the distant circle of the universe where she
was. Because her will had finally been imposed: Her daughter had restored Joaquim Soares da Cunha, that good, timid,
obedient husband and father. All she had had to do was
raise her voice and tighten her face to have him there, sensi-
ble and reconciled. There he was, his hands crossed over his
chest. The tramp had disappeared forever, the "senator of
honky-tonks," the "patriarch of the red-light district."

It was too bad he was dead and couldn't see himself in
the mirror; couldn't witness his daughter's victory, that of
the proper and outraged family.

In that moment of intimate satisfaction, of complete victory, Vanda had wanted to feel generous and good, forgetting the last ten years, as though the competent people
from the funeral parlor had purified them with the same

wet, soapy rag with which they had removed the filth from
Quincas's body. Remembering her childhood, her adoles-
cence, her engagement, her marriage, and the peaceful
image of Joaquim Soares da Cunha, half-hidden in his can-
vas chair reading the newspaper, trembling as Otacília's
voice would call out in reprimand: "Quincas!" That was
how she was thinking about him, feeling tenderness for
him, for that father she had missed, and with a little more
effort she might have been capable of a little sentimentality,
feeling herself an unhappy and desolate orphan.

The room was growing warmer. With the window closed
the sea breeze could find no way to enter. Nor did Vanda
want it: Sea, waterfront, breeze, the streets that climbed up
the hillside, the street noises—they were all part of that
now terminated derangement, its existence ended. All that
should remain there were herself; her dead father, the late
Joaquim Soares da Cunha; and the fondest memories he
had left her. She dug into her past for forgotten episodes.
Her father taking her to a merry-go-round that had been set
up on the Ribeira on the occasion of a feast day at the
church of Bonfim. She had probably never seen anything so
delightful: a grown man up on a child's saddle, bursting
with laughter, he who smiled so little. She also remembered
the tribute his friends and colleagues had paid him when
Joaquim had received a promotion at the Bureau of Revenue. The house was full of people. Vanda was a young girl
then, just starting to date. The one who was all puffed up
with contentment that day was Otacília, in the center of a
group that had formed in the living room, where there were
speeches, beer, and a fountain pen presented to the clerk.
She looked as if she were the one being honored. Joaquim
listened to the speeches, shook hands, and accepted the pen
without showing any great enthusiasm. As though he was
bored by it all and didn't have the courage to say so.

She also remembered her father's face when she told him about Leonardo's impending visit after he had finally decided to ask him for her hand. He had shaken his head and muttered, "Poor devil."

Vanda would brook no criticism of her fiancé. "Why poor devil? He comes from a good family, has a good job, and isn't one for drinking and debauchery."

"I know that, I know that. I was thinking about something else."

It was strange: She couldn't remember many details about her father. It was as if he'd never had an active part in life at home. She could spend hours remembering Otacília: dinners, little things, her expressions, events where her mother was present. The truth is that Joaquim began to figure in their lives only on that absurd day when, after labeling Leonardo a "blockhead," he stared at her and Otacília and out of nowhere threw into their faces, "Vipers!" And with the greatest of calm in the world, as though he were simply carrying out some exceedingly banal act, he left and never came back.

But Vanda didn't want to think about that. She went back to her childhood again. It was there that she found the figure of Joaquim in sharper focus. For example, when she was a girl of five, with hair in braids, and quick to tears, she came down with an alarming fever. Joaquim never left her room, sitting beside the little patient, holding her hands, doling out her medicine. He was a good father and a good husband. With that last memory Vanda felt she had been sufficiently sentimental and—had there been anyone else there at the wake—capable of a bit of weeping, as is the obligation of a good daughter.

With a melancholy look on her face, she stared at the corpse. Polished shoes where the light of the candles gleamed, trousers with a perfect crease, a well-fitting black jacket, devout hands folded over his chest. Her eyes lighted on the shaved chin, and she received her first shock.

She saw the smile. The cynical, immoral smile of someone who was enjoying himself. The smile hadn't changed. The experts from the funeral parlor had been unable to do anything about it. Also she, Vanda, had forgotten to tell them, to ask for an expression more in keeping with the solemnity of the dead. That smile of Quincas Water-Bray's was still there, and in the face of that smile of mockery and pleasure, what good were the new shoes, brand-new while poor Leonardo had to get his half-soled for a second time? What good were the dark suit, the white shirt, the shaved chin, the pomaded hair, the hands placed in prayer? Because Quincas was laughing at all that, a laugh that was growing louder and longer and in a short time would be echoing all over that filthy den. He was laughing with his lips and with his eyes, the eyes staring at the pile of dirty, ragged clothes, tossed in a corner and forgotten by the men from the funeral parlor. The laugh of Quincas Water-Bray.

And Vanda could clearly hear the insulting neatness of the syllables in the funereal silence.

"Viper!"

Vanda was startled. Her eyes flashed like Otacília's, but her face turned pale. That was the word he had used, spitting it out, when she and Otacília had sought him out at the beginning of that madness to lead him back to the comforts of home, his established habits, and his lost decency. Not even now, dead and lying in a coffin, with candles by his feet, dressed in good clothing, would he surrender. He was laughing with his lips and with his eyes. It wouldn't have been all that strange had he started whistling. And, to make matters worse, one of his thumbs—the one on his left hand—wasn't folded properly over his other one but was sticking up, anarchic and taunting.

"Viper!" he said again, and whistled playfully.

Vanda shuddered in her chair and ran her hand over her face. "Can I be going mad?" She felt a need for air; the heat was becoming unbearable, and her head was swimming. Heavy breathing on the stairs: Aunt Marocas, dripping fat, was entering the room. She saw how upset her niece was there on the chair, pale, her eyes fixed on the mouth of the dead man.

"You're all done in, child. And it's so hot in this cubbyhole."

Quincas's devilish smile got wider when he caught sight of his sister's monumental bulk. Vanda wanted to cover her ears. She knew from past experience the words he loved to use to define Marocas, but what good were hands held over her ears in shutting out the voice of a dead man? She heard: "Fart-sack!"

Marocas, recovered now after her climb, opened the window wide without even a glance at the corpse. "Did they put perfume on him? It stinks to high heaven."

The street noises came in through the open window, multiple and merry. The sea breeze put out the candles and drifted over to kiss Quincas on the cheek. The light spread out over him, blue and festive. A victorious smile was on his lips as Quincas settled himself better in the coffin.

7

By that time the news of the unexpected death of Quincas Water-Bray was already circulating through the streets of Bahia. It is quite true that the small merchants at the market didn't close their doors as a sign of mourning. In compensation, however, they immediately raised the price of the Bahian trinkets, straw bags, and clay statuettes that they sold to tourists, paying their homage to the dead man in that way. All about the market there were hurried consultations, something like emergency meetings, with people going back and forth. The news was in the air, going up on the Lacerda Elevator, traveling along on streetcars to Calçada, by bus to Feira de Santana. Lovely black Paula was breaking up in tears at her tapioca-cake stand. Water-Bray wouldn't be coming by that afternoon to whisper his well-chosen come-ons to her, peeking into her ample breasts, propositioning her for wicked things, making her laugh.

On the skiffs with lowered sails the men of the realm of Iemanjá, bronzed sailors, were unable to hide their disappointed surprise: How could that death have taken place in a room in Tabuão? How could the old sailor have given up the ghost in a bed? Hadn't Quincas Water-Bray proclaimed so decisively and so many times with a voice and gesture capable of convincing the strongest doubter that the

only tomb worthy of his roguery was the sea, its endless
waters all bathed in moonlight?

Whenever he found himself the guest of honor on the
poop of a skiff, looking over a sensational fish stew as the
clay pot gave off its fragrant fumes and the bottle of cachaça
went from hand to hand, there was always a moment, as the
guitars began to be plucked, when his maritime instincts
would awaken. He would stand up, his body swaying, the
cachaça giving him that weaving roll of men of the sea, and
he would declare his status of "old sailor." An old sailor
without a sea and without a ship, corrupted on land but
through no fault of his own. For he had been born for the
sea, for hoisting sails and controlling the tiller of skiffs, con-
quering the waves on stormy nights. His destiny had been
cut off, he who could have gotten to be the captain of a ship,
wearing a blue uniform, with a pipe in his mouth. But he
never stopped being a sailor. That was because he had been
born to his mother, Madalena, granddaughter of a ship's
captain. He was maritime from his great-grandfather on
down, and if they had given him that skiff, he would have
been capable of taking it out to sea, not just to Maragogipe
or Cachoeira close-by but also, yes, to the faraway coasts of
Africa in spite of never having sailed. It was in his blood. He
didn't have to learn anything about navigation; he'd been
born with the knowledge. If anyone in that select audience
harbored any doubts, let him step forth. . . . He tipped the
bottle and drank with great gulps. The skiff masters had no
doubts; it could well be the truth. Along the waterfront and
on the beaches, boys were born knowing the things of the
sea. It wasn't worth the trouble to look for explanations.
Then Quincas Water-Bray would make his solemn pledge:
He was reserving the honor of his last hours for the sea, his
final moment. They weren't going to stick him six feet under
the ground—oh no, not that! When his time came he would

demand the freedom of the sea, the journeys he hadn't taken when he was alive, the most daring crossings, unmatched deeds. Master Manuel, without nerves or age, the most daring of the skiff captains, nodded his approval. The others, whom life had taught never to doubt anything, also agreed, taking another swig of booze. The guitars were plucked. They sang to the magic of nights at sea, Janaína's fatal seduction. The "old sailor" was singing louder than all the others.

How could he have died so suddenly in a room in Tabuão? It was beyond belief. The skiff masters heard the news and couldn't come to believe it completely. Quincas Water-Bray was given to hoaxes. He'd put one over on everybody more than once.

The gamblers with their games of fist-guess, three-card monte, and blackjack halted their excited play, dazed, all interest in winning lost. Wasn't Water-Bray their undisputed leader? The late afternoon fell over them like a cloak of deep mourning. In dives, in taverns, over the counters of shops and stores, wherever cachaça was drunk, sadness reigned, and the consumption was directed toward their irremediable loss. Who knew how to drink better than Quincas? He never changed completely. The more firewater he swilled, the more lucid and brilliant he became. Better than anyone else he could guess the brand and the origin of the most diverse drinks, with knowledge of the nuances of color, taste, and aroma in all of them. How long had it been since he had last tasted water? Ever since that day when he came to be called Water-Bray.

Not that it was any memorable event or exciting story, but it's worth telling because it was from that distant day forward that the epithet "Water-Bray" was definitively added to the name Quincas. He had gone into the store owned by López, a pleasant Spaniard, on the outer rim of the market. As a regular customer he had earned the right

to serve himself without the aid of a clerk. On the counter
he spotted a bottle filled to the top with clear cachaça,
transparent and perfect. He filled a glass, spat to clear his
mouth, and tossed it down in one gulp. Then an inhuman
bray cut the morning peace of the market, shaking the very
foundations of the Lacerda Elevator. It was the cry of a
mortally wounded animal, a man who had been betrayed
by an evil fate.

"WAUUUU-TUUH!!!"

Filthy, foul bastard of a Spaniard! People came running
from all around. Someone most certainly was being mur-
dered. The customers in the store were beside themselves
with laughter. That "bray of water" that Quincas gave out
then spread around as a great tale, from the market to
Pelourinho, from the Largo das Sete Portas to the Dique,
from the Calçada to Itapuã. Quincas Water-Bray he
remained from then on, and Quitéria Goggle-Eye, during
moments of great tenderness, would call him "Brayzie"
between her nibbling teeth.

In those houses with the cheapest women too, where
tramps and hooligans, petty smugglers, and beached sailors
found a home, family, and love in the lost hours of the night
after the sad wares of sex when the weary women longed
for a little tenderness, the news of the death of Quincas
Water-Bray brought on desolation and a flow of sad tears.
The women wept as though they'd lost a close relative and
suddenly felt unprotected in their poverty. Some added up
their savings and resolved to buy the prettiest flowers in
Bahia for the dead man. As for Quitéria Goggle-Eye, surrounded by the tearful dedication of her housemates, her
wails cut through the neighborhood of São Miguel to die on
the Largo do Pelourinho. They were heartrending. She
could find consolation only in drink. Between swallows she

would exalt the memory of that unforgettable lover, the most tender and the wildest, the merriest and the wisest.

They remembered things, details and phrases that gave the proper measure of Quincas. He was the one who for over twenty days had taken care of Benedita's three-month-old son when she was in the hospital. All the child was missing was a breast to suckle. Quincas did everything else: changed diapers, cleaned up doo-doo, bathed the baby, gave him his nursing bottle.

Hadn't he jumped in just a few days ago, old and drunk as he was, like a fearless champion, to defend Good Clara when two young perverts, sons of bitches from the best families, tried to beat her up in Viviana's house? And what more pleasant guest than he at the large dining room table at lunchtime? Who knew funnier stories, who could better console the woes of love, who was like a father or an older brother? In the middle of the afternoon Quitéria Goggle-Eye rolled out of her chair and was led to her bed. There she fell asleep with her memories. Several women decided not to look for or to receive any man that night. They were in mourning. As though it were Maundy Thursday or Good Friday.

8

At day's end, as the lights were going on in the city and men were leaving work, Quincas Water-Bray's closest friends— Sparrow, Bangs Blackie, Corporal Martim, and Swifty— were going down the Tabuão hillside on their way to the dead man's room. It must be said in the interest of truth that they weren't drunk yet. They'd had their drinks, of course, with all the commotion brought on by the news, but their eyes were red from the tears they had wept in their measure-less grief, and the same could be said for their garbled speech and wobbly gait. How could they have kept their minds completely clear when a friend of so many years had died, the best of comrades, the most thoroughgoing vagabond in Bahia? As for the bottle that Corporal Martim carried under his shirt, there was never any proof of it.

At that hour of dusk, the mysterious beginning of night, the dead man looked a little weary. Vanda noticed it. Small wonder: He'd spent the whole afternoon laughing, mutter-ing nasty names, making faces. Not even when Leonardo and Uncle Eduardo arrived around five o'clock, not even then did Quincas take a break. He insulted Leonardo with "Dimwit!" and laughed at Eduardo. When the shadows of evening descended over the city, Quincas grew restless. As though he were waiting for something that was late in com-ing. Vanda, in order to forget and to pretend to herself, started up an animated conversation with her husband and her aunt and uncle, avoiding any glance at the dead man. She wanted to go home, get some rest, take a pill to help her sleep. Why were Quincas's eyes going back and forth between the window and the door?

The news hadn't reached the four friends at the same time. The first to find out was Sparrow. He was putting his multiple talents to use advertising shops in the Baixa dos Sapateiros. He was wearing an old, frayed frock coat, his face painted, and he would station himself alongside the door of a shop and, for a miserable pittance, praise its low prices and fine quality, stopping passersby, telling them limp jokes, inviting them in, almost dragging them. Every so often, when his thirst became pressing—the hellish job left his lips and gullet dry—he'd pop over to a bar close-by and have a drink to put his voice back in tune. On one of these back-and-forths he got the news: brutal, like a sock in the belly, leaving him mute. Head down, he went back into the store and told the Syrian that he wouldn't be able to use him anymore that afternoon. Sparrow was still young; joys and sorrows affected him deeply. He couldn't bear that terrible shock all by himself. He needed the company of the other close friends, the usual gang.

The crowds across from the skiff docks, in the Saturday-night market in Água dos Meninos, in Sete Portas, at the capoeira foot-fighting exhibitions on the Estrada da Liberdade, were almost always quite large: sailors, shopkeepers from the market stalls, *babalaô* priests, capoeira fighters, and hooligans, with their long gabbing, adventures, hectic card games, night fishing in the moonlight, wild goings-on in the red-light district. Quincas Water-Bray had many admirers and friends, but those four were the inseparable ones. For year after year they would get together every day, were together every night, with or without money, stuffed with good food or starving to death, sharing drinks, all together in joy and sadness. Only now did Sparrow realize how they were all joined together. Quincas's death was like an amputation for him; it was as though someone had stolen an arm, a leg, had torn out an eye. That eye in the heart that the priestess Senhora, mistress of all wisdom, spoke about. All together, Sparrow thought, was how they should put in an appearance at Quincas's wake.

He went off to look for Bangs Blackie, at that hour most certainly on the Largo das Sete Portas helping out numbers bankers and putting together a little change for his night-time cachaça. Bangs Blackie stood over six feet tall, and when he puffed out his chest he looked like a statue, so big and strong was he. No one could beat him when he was mad. Fortunately, that rarely happened, because Bangs Blackie was jolly and good-hearted.

Sparrow found him on the Largo das Sete Portas, just as he had figured. There he was, sitting on the pavement by the small market, drenched in tears, clutching an almost empty bottle. Next to him, in the solidarity of grief and cachaça, were several vagabonds, making up a chorus for his lamentations and sighs. He'd already heard the news, as Sparrow could see as soon as he took in the scene. Bangs Blackie would toss down a drink, wipe away a tear, and roar with despair, "Our father, the father of the people, has died . . ."

". . . father of the people . . . ," the others moaned.

The consoling bottle was passed around, and tears formed in the black man's eyes as his suffering grew greater.

"The good man has died . . ."

". . . the good man . . ."

From time to time a new element would join the group, sometimes without knowing what it was all about. Bangs Blackie would pass him the bottle and let out the cry of someone who had been stabbed.

"He was so good . . ."

". . . so good . . . ," repeated the others, except for the newcomer, who was waiting for an explanation for the lamentations and the free cachaça.

"You say it too, damn you." Bangs Blackie, without standing up, stuck out his powerful arm and was shaking the newcomer, an angry gleam in his eyes. "Or do you think he was no good?"

Someone hurried to explain before things got ugly.

"It was Quincas Water-Bray who died."

"Quincas? He *was* a good man," the new member of the chorus said, both convinced and terrified.

"Another bottle!" Bangs Blackie demanded between sobs.

An agile little black boy jumped up and ran to a nearby stall. "Bangs wants another bottle."

Wherever the news arrived, Quincas's death increased the consumption of cachaça. Sparrow was observing the scene from a distance. The news had traveled faster than he had. The black man saw him too and gave out with a fearsome roar, lifting his hands up to the sky, standing up.

"Sparrow, little brother, our father, the father of the people, is dead."

". . . our father, the father of the people . . . ," the chorus repeated.

"Shut up, you bastards. Let me give my little brother Sparrow a hug."

They observed the rites of courtesy of the people of Bahia, from the poorest to those properly brought up. Mouths fell silent. Sparrow's coattails were flapping in the breeze; the tears began to run down his painted face. Bangs Blackie and he embraced three times, their sobs mingling. Sparrow drank from the new bottle, seeking consolation in it. Bangs Blackie wasn't finding any consolation.

"The light of the night has gone out . . ."

". . . the light of the night . . ."

Sparrow proposed, "Let's go find the others and pay him a visit."

Corporal Martim might be in any of three or four places. Either sleeping at Carmela's, still tired from the night before, chatting by the market docks, or playing cards in the Água dos Meninos market. Martim had dedicated himself to those three occupations only after he was discharged from the army some fifteen years earlier: love, conversation, gambling. He'd never followed any other known trade, with women and fools providing him with enough to live on. To work after having worn his glorious uniform would have been an obvious humiliation for Corporal Martim. His haughty pride of a handsome mulatto and the agility of his hands with a deck of cards brought him respect. Not to mention his skill on the guitar.

He was exhibiting his way with cards at the Água dos Meninos market. By doing it with such ease, he was contributing to the spiritual happiness of bus and truck drivers, playing a part in the education of two black urchins just beginning their practical apprenticeship in life, and helping any number of vendors to spend the profits they had made from their sales that day in the market stalls. In that way he was undertaking work of the most praiseworthy kind. It goes unexplained, then, why one of the vendors wasn't all that enthusiastic about Martim's virtuosity in dealing, as the man kept muttering, "Luck like that's got a fishy smell about it." Corporal Martim raised his eyes, brimming with blue innocence at the hasty critic, passed him the deck to deal if he wanted to and if he thought he had the necessary competence. As for himself, Corporal Martim preferred to bet against the bank, breaking it and reducing the banker to the most abject poverty. And he would not tolerate insinuations

concerning his honesty. As an old soldier he was particularly
sensitive to whispers that cast doubt on his upright character. So sensitive was he that any new provocation would
oblige him to bust somebody in the face. The enthusiasm of
the urchins grew; the drivers rubbed their hands together,
all excited. Nothing better than a good fight, spontaneous
and unexpected like that. Just when everything was all set to
start, Sparrow and Bangs Blackie appeared, bearing the
tragic news and the bottle of cachaça, with just a tiny bit left
in it. They were already shouting to the corporal from a distance.

"He died! He died!"

Corporal Martim stared at them, his good eye lingering
on the bottle with quick calculations, and he commented to
the group, "Something important must have happened for
them to have drunk a whole bottle already. Either Bangs
Blackie hit the numbers or Sparrow's got himself engaged."

As Sparrow was an incurable romantic, he was always
getting engaged, the victim of his explosive passions. Every
engagement was properly celebrated, with joy at the beginning and with philosophical sadness when it ended a short
time later.

"Somebody died," a trucker said.

Corporal Martim listened hard.

"He died! He died!"

The two of them were coming along all hunched over
with the weight of the news. From Sete Portas to Água dos
Meninos, passing by the skiff docks and Carmela's house,
they'd given the sad news to a lot of people. Why was it that
every one of them, on learning about Quincas's passing,
immediately uncorked a bottle? It wasn't their fault, heralds
of grief and mourning, that there were so many people
along the way, that Quincas had so many friends and
acquaintances. Drinking in the city of Bahia began much

earlier than usual on that day. It couldn't be helped. It wasn't every day that a Quincas Water-Bray died.

Corporal Martim, forgetting about the fight and with the cards still in his hand, was watching them with increasing curiosity. They were crying—that was obvious. Bangs Blackie's voice was all choked up.

"Our father, the father of the people, has died . . ."

"Was it Jesus Christ or the governor?" asked one of the black urchins, who had the reputation of a jokester. The black man reached out his hand and flung him to the ground.

They could all understand that it was a serious matter. Sparrow raised the bottle and said, "Water-Bray has died!"

The deck of cards dropped from Martim's hand. The suspicious vendor saw his worst fears confirmed—aces and queens—as the dealer's cards scattered all over. But the name of Quincas had reached his ears too. He decided not to argue. Corporal Martim asked Sparrow for the bottle, then threw it away with disdain. He stood for a long time looking at the market stalls, the trucks and buses on the street, the boats in the bay, the people coming and going. He got the feeling of a sudden emptiness, couldn't hear the birds in the cages nearby in a vendor's stall.

He wasn't a man for weeping; a soldier doesn't cry, even after he's put aside his uniform. But his eyes grew tiny, his voice changed, he lost all his bluster. It was almost with the voice of a child that he asked, "How could it have happened?"

After picking up his cards, he joined the other two. They still had to look for Swifty. He had no certain perch, except on Thursday and Sunday afternoons when invariably he would be performing in Valdemar's capoeira ring on the Estrada da Liberdade. Outside of that, his profession carried him off to distant places. He hunted for rats and toads to sell to laboratories for medical tests and scientific

experiments—which made Swifty a figure to be admired in
the opinion of the most respected people. Wasn't he a bit of a
scientist himself? Didn't he talk to doctors, know big words?

Only after lots of walking and drinking did they come
upon him, all wrapped up in his big coat as though it were
cold, mumbling to himself. He'd gotten the news through
other channels, and he was also looking for his friends.
When he met them he put his hand into one of his pockets.
To take out a handkerchief to wipe away his tears, Sparrow
thought. But out of the depths of his pocket Swifty had
pulled a small green bullfrog, gleaming like an emerald.

"I was keeping it for Quincas. I never found one so
pretty."

9

When they appeared at the door of the room, Swifty thrust out his hand, in the extended palm of which rested the frog with its bulging eyes. They stayed there standing in the doorway, one behind the other. Bangs Blackie stuck in his big head to take a look. Swifty, embarrassed, put the creature back in his pocket.

The family halted their animated conversation. Four pairs of hostile eyes stared at the shabby group. That's all we needed, thought Vanda. Corporal Martim, who in matters of etiquette was second only to Quincas himself, took off his filthy cap and greeted those present.

"Good evening, ladies and gentlemen. We just wanted to view him."

He took a step inside. The others followed. The family backed away. They had been standing around the coffin. Sparrow got the thought that it was a trick, that the dead man wasn't Quincas Water-Bray. He recognized him by only his smile. The four of them were dumbfounded. They never could have imagined Quincas so clean and elegant, so well dressed. They instantly lost their self-assurance, and their tipsiness disappeared as if by magic. The presence of the family—the women especially—left them fearful and timid, not knowing how to act, where to put their hands, how to behave before the dead man.

Sparrow, so ridiculous with his face painted red and wearing his shabby frock coat, looked at the other three, suggesting that they get away from there as fast as possible. Corporal Martim was hesitating, like a general on the eve of battle, assessing the enemy's strength. Swifty made a step toward the door. Only Bangs Blackie, still bringing up the rear, lifting his big head up to see, didn't hesitate for a second. Quincas was smiling at him, and the black man smiled back. There was no human force capable of dragging him away from there, from beside little Papa Quincas. He grabbed Swifty by the arm, answered Sparrow's request with his eyes. Corporal Martim understood; a soldier doesn't flee the field of battle. The four of them drew back from the coffin to a corner of the room.

There they all were now, in silence: on one side the family of Joaquim Soares da Cunha—daughter, son-in-law, brother, and sister—and on the other side the friends of Quincas Water-Bray. Swifty put his hand into his pocket and felt the frightened frog, as though he wanted to show it to Quincas. With a movement that looked like ballet, the friends drew back from the coffin and the relatives drew closer. Vanda cast a glance of reproach at her father. Even in death he preferred the company of those ragamuffins.

Quincas had been waiting for them. He had grown restless as the afternoon ended, because the vagabonds were late in getting there. Just when Vanda had begun to think her father had been defeated and was finally ready to surrender, to silence the foul words on his lips, defeated by the silent, dignified resistance she had put up to all his provocations, that smile was gleaming once again on the dead face, and more than ever it was the corpse of Quincas Water-Bray that lay before her. Had it not been an offense to Otacília's memory, she would have left off her mourning and dumped the unworthy body somewhere in Tabuão, given the barely used coffin back to the funeral parlor, and sold the new clothes to some old-clothes peddler at half price. The silence was becoming unbearable.

Leonardo turned to his wife and her aunt. "I think it's time you two got going. It'll be getting late pretty soon."

Just a few moments before, all Vanda wanted to do was go home and get some rest. She gritted her teeth. She wasn't a woman to give in, and she replied, "In a little while."

Bangs Blackie sat down on the floor and leaned his head against the wall. Swifty nudged him with his foot. It wasn't right to settle down like that in the presence of the dead man's family. Corporal Martim showed his admonishment by staring at the black man. Bangs lifted his hand and pushed his friend's annoying foot away as he sobbed, "He was our father! Papa Quincas . . ."

It was like a punch in the belly for Vanda, a slap in the face for Leonardo, a spit in the eye for Eduardo. Only Aunt Marocas laughed, her fat quivering as she sat in the only, and disputed, chair.

"How amusing!"

Bangs Blackie went from tears to laughter, taken with Marocas. Even more startling than his sobs was the black man's hearty laugh. It was like a thunderclap in the room, and Vanda heard another laugh behind Blackie's: Quincas was enjoying himself enormously.

"What sort of disrespect is that?" Her dry voice put an end to that beginning of cordiality.

With the reprimand, Aunt Marocas got up, took a few steps about the room, followed always by the admiration of Bangs Blackie as he looked her over from head to toe, finding her to be a woman to his taste: a bit old, that's true, but big and fat, the way he liked them. He didn't like those skinny little ones whose waists you couldn't even pinch. If Bangs Blackie could have run into that madame on the beach, the two of them would have had a ball; all you had to do was take one look at her and you'd see her virtues right off. Aunt Marocas began to mention her wish to leave. She felt tired and nervous. Vanda, having taken back her place on the chair by the coffin, made no reply. She had the look of a guard watching over a treasure.

"We're all tired," Eduardo said.

"It would be best if they left." Leonardo had his fears about the Tabuão neighborhood at night, when all commercial activity ceased and the prostitutes and street people took over.

Well-mannered, as was his way, and wishing to cooperate, Corporal Martim proposed, "If you good people would like to go get some rest and a little shut-eye, we'll stay on here and watch over him."

Eduardo knew that wouldn't be right: They shouldn't leave the corpse alone with those people, with no family member present. But he would like to accept the proposal— oh, how he would: All day at the store, going back and forth, taking care of customers, giving orders to the help—it dragged a man down. Eduardo went to bed early and got up with the dawn, a strict timetable. When he got home from the store, after a bath and dinner, he would sit down in a chaise longue, stretch out his legs, and immediately fall asleep. That brother of his, Quincas, knew only how to be a nuisance. For ten years that's all he'd been. That night he was obliging him to stay on his feet, having nothing but a couple sandwiches to eat. Why not leave him with his friends, that gang of tramps, the people he'd been hanging out with for ten years? What were he and Marocas, Vanda, and Leonardo doing there in that filthy hole, that rat's nest? He didn't have the courage to express his thoughts: Vanda was spoiled; she was quite capable of reminding him of the many times that he, Eduardo, starting out in life, had had recourse to Quincas's wallet. He looked at Corporal Martim with a certain benevolence.

Swifty, defeated in his attempts to get Bangs Blackie to stand up, sat down too. He had the urge to put the frog in the palm of his hand and play with it. He'd never seen one that beautiful. Sparrow, who'd spent part of his childhood in a children's home run by priests, searched his dull memory for a complete prayer. He'd always heard it said that the dead stood in need of prayers. And priests . . . Had the priest been there already, or was he coming only on the next day? The question was tickling his throat. He couldn't resist.

"Has the priest come already?"

"Tomorrow morning," Marocas replied.

Vanda scolded her with her eyes: Why start a conversation with that riffraff? But having gained her respect, Vanda felt better. She exiled the vagabonds to a corner of the room, made them keep quiet. However, it would be impossible for her to spend the night there. Neither she nor Aunt Marocas. She had the vague hope at first that Quincas's indecent friends wouldn't stay long, as there was neither food nor drink. She didn't know why they were still there in the room. It couldn't have been out of friendship for the dead man; those people don't maintain friendships with anyone. In any case, even the disagreeable presence of friends like that was of no importance, because they wouldn't be at the burial the next day. She, Vanda, would take charge of the events, and the family would be alone with the corpse once more. They would bury Joaquim Soares da Cunha with modesty and dignity.

She arose from the chair and called to Marocas: "Let's go." And to Leonardo: "Don't stay too late. You can't spend the whole night. Uncle Eduardo has already said he'd stay the whole time."

Eduardo, taking over the chair, agreed. Leonardo went along to see them to the streetcar. Corporal Martim ventured a "Good night, ladies," but got no response. Only the candles were lighting up the room. Bangs Blackie was sleeping, giving off a fearsome snore.

10

At ten o'clock Leonardo got up from the kerosene can and went over to the candles, looking at his watch. He woke up Eduardo, who was sleeping with his mouth open, uncomfortable in the chair.

"I'm leaving. I'll be back in the morning, at six, to give you some time to go home and change your clothes."

Eduardo stretched his legs, thinking about his bed. His neck hurt. In the corner of the room Sparrow, Swifty, and Corporal Martim were talking in low voices, having a heated argument: Which one of them was going to take Quincas's place in Quitéria Goggle-Eye's bed? Corporal Martim, exhibiting a revolting selfishness, would not accept being scratched from the list just because he was in possession of the heart and the slim body of little black Carmela. When the sound of Leonardo's steps had disappeared onto the street, Eduardo looked at the group. The argument came to a halt. Corporal Martim smiled at the storekeeper. The latter was looking with envy at Bangs Blackie, lost in the best of sleeps. He settled himself in the chair again and put his feet on the kerosene can. His neck still hurt. Swifty couldn't resist. He took the frog out of his pocket and put it on the floor. It took a leap. It was funny. It looked like a spook loose in the room. Eduardo couldn't manage any sleep. He looked at the dead man, motionless in the coffin.

He was the only one who was comfortably lying down. What the devil was he, Eduardo, doing there playing watchman? Wasn't it enough to go to the burial? Wasn't he paying part of the expenses? He was going beyond his brotherly duties, especially for a brother like Quincas, who was an annoyance to his life.

He stood up and moved his limbs about, opened his mouth in a yawn. Swifty was hiding the little green frog in his hand. Sparrow was thinking about Quitéria Goggle-Eye. A woman and lots of it. . . .

Eduardo turned to face them. "Tell me something . . ."

Corporal Martim, a psychologist by nature and by necessity, came to attention. "At your orders, commandant, sir." Who knows, maybe the merchant would send out for some drinks to help pass the long night.

"Are you all planning to spend the night here?"

"With him? Yes, sir. We were friends."

"Then I'm going to go home and get a little rest." He put his hand in his pocket and took out a bill. The eyes of the corporal, Sparrow, and Swifty were following his movements. "Here's something for you to buy some sandwiches with. But don't leave him alone, not for one minute, eh?"

"You can rest easy. We'll keep him company."

Before they began their drinking, Sparrow and Swifty lit cigarettes and Corporal Martim one of those fifty-centavo cigars, black and strong, the kind only real smokers could appreciate. The powerful smoke passed across the black man's nostrils, but not even then did Bangs wake up. As soon as they uncorked the cachaça (the disputed first bottle that, according to the family, the corporal had brought in under his shirt), Bangs Blackie opened his eyes and demanded a drink.

The first round brought out a critical spirit in the four

friends. That stuck-up family of Quincas's had shown itself to be stingy and greedy. They did everything halfway. Where were the chairs for visitors to sit in? Where were the usual food and drink they have at poor people's wakes? Martim had served as watch for many wakes. He'd never seen one with such a lack of activity. Even at the poorest of them, they served at least coffee and a swig of cachaça. Quincas didn't deserve such treatment. What did it get them to belch out their importance and then leave the dead man in that humiliation, with nothing to offer his friends? Sparrow and Swifty went to get something to sit on and some food. Corporal Martim thought it necessary at least to organize the wake with a minimum of decorum. Sitting in the chair, he gave orders: some crates and bottles. Bangs Blackie was on the kerosene can, and he nodded his approval.

It must be confessed, however, that with regard to the corpse itself, the family had behaved quite well. New clothes, new shoes—all of it elegant. And nice candles, the church kind. Even so, they'd forgotten the flowers. Where did you ever see a corpse without flowers?

"He looks like a gentleman," Bangs Blackie said proudly. "An elegant dead man!"

Quincas smiled at the praise.

The black man returned his smile. "Little Papa . . . ," he said, lovingly poking him in the ribs, the way he used to when he'd just heard one of Quincas's good stories.

Sparrow and Swifty returned with some crates, a chunk of salami, and some full bottles. They stood in a semicircle around the dead man, and then Sparrow suggested they say an Our Father together. He managed, with a surprising effort of memory, to remember the prayer almost in its entirety. The others followed along, showing little conviction. It didn't look all that easy for them. Bangs Blackie knew

some drumbeats for Oxum and Oxalá, but his religious
training hadn't gone much further than that. It had been
some thirty years since the last time Swifty had prayed. Corporal Martim considered prayers and churches weaknesses,
not very much in keeping with military life. Even so, they
made an attempt, with Sparrow leading the prayer and the
others responding as best they could. Finally, Sparrow, who
had knelt and lowered his head in contrition, grew annoyed.

"You bunch of boobs!"

"A lack of training," the corporal explained. "But it did
amount to something. The priest will take care of the rest
tomorrow."

Quincas seemed indifferent to the prayer. It must have
been hot for him in those heavy clothes. Bangs Blackie
looked his friend over. They had to do something for him
now, because the prayer hadn't worked. Should they sing a
chant from *candomblé* maybe? They had to do something.
He asked Swifty, "Where's the toad? Take him out."

"He's not a toad; he's a frog. What good will he be?"

"Maybe Quincas will like him."

Swifty carefully took out the frog and placed him on
Quincas's crossed hands. The animal leaped and nestled
himself in the bottom of the coffin. When the wavy light
from the candles hit his body, green flashes of light ran over
the corpse.

The argument over Quitéria Goggle-Eye started up again.
Sparrow was more combative after a few drinks. He raised
his voice in defense of his interests.

Bangs Blackie complained: "Aren't you two ashamed to
be arguing about his woman in front of him? Him still
warm and you like a couple of vultures."

"He's the one who should decide," Swifty said. He was
hopeful that Quincas would choose him to inherit Quitéria,

his only possession. Hadn't he just brought him the prettiest green frog he'd ever caught?

"Unh!" said the dead man.

"You see? He doesn't like this talk," the black man scolded.

"Let's give him a drink too," the corporal proposed, desirous to be in the dead man's good graces.

They opened his mouth and poured in the cachaça. A little spilled onto his coat collar and shirtfront.

"I never saw anyone drink on his back."

"It would be best to prop him up. Then he can look right at us."

They sat Quincas up in the coffin, his head lolling from one side to the other. With the swig of cachaça his smile had grown broader.

"Nice jacket," Corporal Martim said, examining the material. "It's foolish to put new clothes on a dead man. He died, he's finished, he's going six feet under. New clothes for the worms to eat while there are so many people in need . . ."

Words full of truth, they thought. They gave Quincas another drink. The dead man nodded. He was a man who could agree with someone who was right. He was obviously in agreement with what Martim had been saying.

"He's ruining the clothes."

"It would be better if we took off the jacket so it won't get all messed up."

Quincas seemed relieved when they took off the heavy, hot, black coat jacket. But since he was still spitting up cachaça, they took his shirt off too. Sparrow had fallen in love with the shiny shoes. His were a shamble. What does a dead man need with new shoes, eh, Quincas?

"They're just the right size for my feet," said Sparrow.

Bangs Blackie picked up his friend's old clothes, which had been lying in a corner of the room, and together they put them on him. Then they recognized him.

"There now. Yes, that's the old Quincas."

They felt happy. Quincas seemed happier too, rid of those uncomfortable clothes. He was especially grateful to Sparrow because the shoes had been pinching his feet. The street peddler took advantage of this and put his mouth close to Quincas's ear, whispering something about Quitéria. What had he done that for? Bangs Blackie had been right that talk about the whore would irritate Quincas. He became violent, spitting out a gush of cachaça into Sparrow's ear. The others shuddered, scared.

"He's mad."

"What did I tell you?"

Swifty finished putting on the new shoes. Corporal Martim got the jacket. Bangs Blackie would exchange the shirt for a bottle of cachaça in a shop he knew. They were sorry he didn't have any underwear on. Corporal Martim spoke quite to the point when he said to Quincas, "I don't mean to say anything bad, but that family of yours is a tad stingy. I think your son-in-low made off with your underwear."

"Tightwads," Quincas corrected.

"Since you say so yourself, it must be true. We didn't mean to offend them. After all, they *are* your relatives. But so stingy, so chinchy . . . buying our own drinks. Where did you ever see a wake like this?"

"Not even a single flower," Blackie agreed. "I'm glad I haven't got relatives like that lot."

"The men are blockheads and the women vipers," Quincas defined with precision.

"Look, little Papa, the chubby one might be worth a few puffs. She's got a nice rear end."

"A fart-sack."

"Don't say that, little Papa. She may be a little on the fat side, but that's no reason to put her down. I've seen worse."

"You dumb nigger, you couldn't tell a pretty woman if you were looking right at her."

Swifty, with no sense of the proper moment, spoke up. "Quitéria's pretty, isn't she, old man? What's she going to do now? I was thinking . . ."

"Shut your mouth, you bastard! Can't you see he's getting mad?"

But Quincas wasn't listening. He had turned his head toward Corporal Martim, who at that very moment was trying to steal his turn in the distribution of drinks. Quincas almost knocked the bottle over with his head.

"Give little Papa his cachaça," Bangs Blackie demanded.

"He was spilling it," the corporal explained.

"He can drink it any way he wants to. That's his right."

Corporal Martim put the bottle to Quincas's open mouth. "Take it easy, old chum. I wasn't trying to cheat you. There you are. Drink all you want. It's your party, after all."

They'd dropped the argument over Quitéria. From the looks of it, Quincas wouldn't even let them mention the matter.

"Good stuff!" Sparrow praised.

"Crummy!" corrected Quincas, a connoisseur.

"A good price too."

The frog had leaped onto Quincas's chest. Quincas was admiring it. It didn't take long for him to tuck it away in the pocket of his old, greasy coat.

The moon had come up over the city and its waters. The Bahia moon, with its flow of silver, was coming in through the window. The sea breeze came in along with it and put out the candles. You couldn't see the coffin anymore. The melody from some guitars was coming down the hillside;

the voice of a woman was singing the sorrows of love. Corporal Martim began singing too.

"He loved to hear a good song . . ."

All four of them were singing. Bangs Blackie's bass voice carried on down beyond the hillside to where the skiffs were. They were drinking and singing. Quincas didn't miss a single swig or a single note. He liked music.

When they'd had their fill of all the singing, Sparrow asked, "Wasn't tonight the night for Master Manuel's *moqueca* fish stew?"

"Right. Today. A *moqueca* with ray fish," Swifty emphasized.

"Nobody can make *moqueca* like Maria Clara," the corporal affirmed.

Quincas stuck out his tongue. Bangs Blackie laughed. "He's crazy about *moqueca*."

"So why don't we go? Master Manuel might be offended."

They looked at one another. They would already be a little late because they still had to pick up the women.

Sparrow expressed some doubt. "We promised not to leave him all alone."

"All alone? What do you mean? He's coming with us."

"I'm hungry," said Bangs Blackie.

They consulted Quincas.

"Do you want to come?"

"You think I'm a cripple, staying behind here?"

After a drink to empty the bottle, they stood Quincas up. Bangs Blackie commented, "He's so drunk he can't handle it. At his age he's losing his capacity for cachaça. Let's go, little Papa."

Sparrow and Swifty went ahead. Quincas, satisfied with life, was doing a dance step between Bangs Blackie and Corporal Martim, holding their arms.

11

From the way things were going, it was looking to be a memorable, even unforgettable, night. Quincas Water-Bray was having one of his best days. An unusual enthusiasm came over the group—they felt themselves to be the lords of that fantastic night, with the moon wrapping the city of Bahia in mystery. On the Ladeira do Pelourinho, couples hid in ancient doorways, cats yowled on roofs, guitars wailed their serenades. It was a night of enchantment, as distant drumbeats sounded and the Pelourinho, where the pillory once stood, looked like a phantasmagoric stage set.

Quincas Water-Bray, enjoying himself mightily, was trying to trip up the corporal and the black man. He was sticking out his tongue at passersby and tipping his head into doorways for a leer at lovers. With every step he took, he felt like lying down on the street. The five friends had lost their sense of haste. It was as though time belonged to them completely, like they were beyond the bounds of any calendar and that magical Bahian night would last for at least a week. Because, as Bangs Blackie affirmed, the birthday of Quincas Water-Bray couldn't be celebrated in the short span of a few hours. Quincas hadn't denied it was his birthday in spite of the fact they weren't too sure when they had celebrated it in previous years. But they had celebrated, that was for sure, Sparrow's multiple engagements, the birthdays of Maria Clara and Quitéria, and, once, a scientific discovery by one of Swifty's customers. In the joy of his accomplishment, the scientist had placed a bill of fifty in the hand of his "humble collaborator." As for Quincas's birthday, it might be the first time they would be celebrating it, and they had to do it right. They were going along the Ladeira do Pelourinho on their way to Quitéria's house.

It was strange: There wasn't the usual bustle in the bars and bawdy houses of São Miguel. Everything was different that night. Could there have been an unexpected police raid, shutting down the houses, locking up the bars? Had detectives taken Quitéria, Carmela, Doralice, Ernestina, and fat Margarida away? Might they be ending up in a trap too? Corporal Martim assumed command of the operation. Sparrow went ahead on a spying mission.

"You scout it out," the corporal explained.

They sat down to wait on the steps of a church on the square. There was still a bottle to finish. Quincas was lying down, looking at the sky, smiling in the moonlight.

Sparrow returned, accompanied by a noisy crowd that was cheering and shouting. Easily recognized at the head of the group was the majestic figure of Quitéria Goggle-Eye, all dressed in black with a mantilla over her head, an inconsolable widow, supported by two women.

"Where is he? Where is he?" she was shouting, all excited.

Sparrow ran ahead and clambered up the steps. In his ragged coat he looked like a speaker at a street rally as he explained, "The news has got around about Water-Bray kicking the bucket. Everything's all in mourning."

Quincas and his friends laughed.

"He's here, people. It's his birthday, and we're celebrating it. We're on our way to a fish dinner on Master Manuel's skiff."

Quitéria Goggle-Eye freed herself from the comforting

arms of Doralice and fat Margô and tried to drop down to where Quincas was sitting on a church step next to Bangs Blackie. But—due to the emotion of that supreme moment, no doubt—Quitéria lost her balance and fell backward on her ass on the stone steps. They immediately lifted her up and helped her get closer.

"You bandit! You dog! Damn you! What's the big idea, spreading the news that you've died, getting everybody all worked up?"

She sat down beside Quincas, smiling. She took his hand and placed it over her ample breast so he could feel the beating of her afflicted heart.

"I almost died from the news, and here you are, off on a binge, you devil you. Who can keep up with you, Brayzie, you devil, so full of tricks? You hurt me, Brayzie, you were killing me."

The group was laughing at it all. In bars the tumult picked up again. Life returned to the Ladeira de São Miguel. They continued on their way to Quitéria's house. Quitéria was beautiful, all dressed in black like that. She'd never looked so desirable to them.

As they went along the Ladeira de São Miguel on their way to the brothel, they bathed in all manner of demonstrations of thanks. At the Flower of São Miguel, Hansen the German offered them a round of drinks. Farther along the Frenchman Verger passed out African amulets for the women. He was unable to go along with them because he still had an obligation to a saint to fulfill that night. The doors of the brothels opened up again, and women reappeared at the windows and on the sidewalk. Wherever they went, they heard shouts for Quincas, people cheering his name. He was nodding his thanks like a king returning to his realm. At Quitéria's house everything was in mourning and sadness. On the bureau in her bedroom, alongside a

print of Our Lord of Bonfim and the clay statue of the
Indian Aroeira, her guide, a picture of Quincas clipped out
of the newspaper—from a series of articles by Giovanni
Guimarães on the "underground life of Bahia"—was in a
prominent position between two lighted candles, with a red
rose beneath it. Doralice, Quitéria's housemate, had already
opened a bottle and was serving drinks in blue wineglasses.
Quitéria blew out the candles. Quincas was lying on the
bed while the others went out into the dining room. Quitéria wasn't long before joining them.

"The bastard fell asleep on me."

"He's on a mother of a bender," Swifty explained.

"Let him get some sleep," Bangs Blackie advised. "He's
had a rough day. He's a right to . . ."

But they were already late for Master Manuel's fish dinner, and after a while the feeling was to wake Quincas up.
Quitéria, black Carmela, and fat Margarida would go with
them. Doralice couldn't accept the invitation. She'd just gotten word from Dr. Carmino. He was coming by that night.
And Dr. Carmino, as they were all aware, paid by the month.
It was guaranteed. She couldn't disappoint him.

They went down the hill, hurrying now. Quincas was
almost running, stumbling over the cobblestones, dragging
along Quitéria and Bangs Blackie as he clutched them. They
hoped they could get there in time to find the skiff still at
the dock.

They made one stop, however, at Cazuza's bar. Cazuza
was an old friend. There were never many people in that
bar, and a night didn't go by when there wasn't some fracas
or other. A gang of pot smokers hung out there every day.
But Cazuza was a nice man, and he'd serve drinks on the
cuff, even a whole bottle. And since they couldn't arrive at
the skiff empty-handed, they decided to have a little chat
with Cazuza and get three quarts of cane liquor. While

Corporal Martim, an irresistible diplomat, was whispering over the bar to the owner, who was stupefied to see Quincas Water-Bray in the best of shape, the others sat down with something to whet their appetites, on the house in honor of the birthday boy. The bar was full with a bunch of morose young men, some jolly sailors, women down to their last penny, and intercity bus drivers who were leaving for Feira de Santana that night.

The fight was unexpected, and it was a beauty. Truth be told, Quincas was the cause of it. He was sitting with his head resting on Quitéria's breast and his legs stretched out. The story goes that one of the young squirts tripped over Quincas's legs as he passed by and almost took a tumble. He made a nasty remark. Bangs Blackie didn't like the pothead's attitude. Quincas had every right to be exactly where he was that night, even stretching his legs out any way he felt like. And he told him so. If the young fellow hadn't reacted, nothing would have happened. But moments later another from the same group of pot smokers tried to get by too. He asked Quincas to move his legs. Quincas pretended not to hear him. Then the skinny guy gave him a hard shove and cursed him. Quincas bumped him with his head, and the fun began. Bangs Blackie grabbed the kid, as was his custom, and tossed him onto another table. The pot smokers got fighting mad and advanced. What happened then is impossible to describe. All anyone could see was Quitéria up on a chair, beautiful, with a bottle in her hand, swinging her arm. Corporal Martim assumed command.

At the end of the fight—a total victory for Quincas's friends and the bus drivers who took their side—Swifty had a black eye; a tail of Sparrow's frock coat had been ripped, quite a serious piece of damage; and Quincas was stretched out on the ground. He'd taken some hard punches and had hit his head on the floor tiles. The potheads had fled. Quitéria was bending over Quincas, trying to bring him around. Cazuza was looking on philosophically from behind the bar at chair legs sticking up in the air, overturned tables, and broken glasses. He was used to that, and the news would increase his fame and the number of customers in the place. He himself was not beyond appreciating a good fight.

Even Quincas came to after a good swig. He continued drinking in that strange way of his, spitting out part of the cachaça wastefully. If it hadn't been Quincas's birthday, Corporal Martim would have gracefully brought it to his attention. They headed for the docks.

By then Master Manuel was no longer waiting for them. He'd finished the fish dinner, which they'd eaten right there by the dock, and he didn't want to go out beyond the break-water with just a bunch of sailors crowded around the clay pot. Deep down he'd never believed the news of Quincas's death, and so he wasn't surprised to see Quincas arm in arm with Quitéria. The Old Sailor couldn't die on land in just any old bed.

"There's still enough ray fish for everybody."

They unfurled the sails of the skiff and hauled up the big stone they used as an anchor. The moon had turned the sea into a silver pathway, at the end of which the darkened city of Bahia stood outlined against the mountain. The skiff was slowly moving off. Maria Clara's voice rose up in a sea chanty:

> *'Twas in the depths of the sea I found you,*
> *All dressed up in your cockleshells . . .*

They clustered around the steaming kettle. The clay dishes were filling up with the sweetest-smelling ray you ever tasted. A *moqueca* with *dendê* oil and pepper. The bottle of cachaça was making its rounds. Corporal Martim was never one to lose sight of the important things. Even during his command of the combat, he had managed to sneak a few bottles under the women's skirts. Quitéria and Quincas were the only ones not eating, as they lay at the stern of the skiff listening to Maria Clara's song. The goggle-eyed beauty was whispering words of love into the Old Sailor's ear.

"Why did you give us such a fright, you devil of a Bray-boy you? You know very well that I've got a weak heart. The doctor warned me against getting too upset. What gave you the idea I could go on living without you, you sharpie, you lowlife? I'm used to you, to your crazy antics, to your wise old age, to your way of not having any way, to how you like to be such a nice fellow. Why did you do this to me today?" And she took the head that had been hurt in the fight and kissed his wicked eyes.

Quincas didn't reply. He was breathing in the sea air as one of his hands touched the water and raised a small wake in the waves. Everything was so peaceful as the party began: Maria Clara's voice, the beauty of the fish stew, the breeze that had become a wind, the moon up in the sky, Quitéria's whispering. But then some unexpected clouds came from the south and swallowed up the full moon. The stars began to be snuffed out, and the wind grew cold and dangerous.

Master Manuel advised, "It's going to be a stormy night. We'd better get back."

He intended to get the skiff back to port before the storm broke. But the cachaça was pleasant and the talk agreeable, there was still a lot of ray fish in the kettle floating in the yellow of the *dendê* oil, and Maria Clara's voice was filling the air with sadness and a desire to linger on the water some more. Besides, how could they break up the idyll of Quincas and Quitéria on that night of celebration?

So it was that the storm, its whistling winds and curling waves, caught them still out. The lights of Bahia were shining in the distance. A bolt of lightning flashed in the darkness. The rain began to fall. Sucking on his pipe, Master Manuel went back to the tiller.

No one knows how it was that Quincas stood up and leaned against the smaller mast. Quitéria didn't take her eyes off the figure of the Old Sailor as he smiled at the waves washing over the skiff, at the flashes lighting up the darkness. Men and women tied themselves to the hawsers, clutched the gunwales of the skiff, as the wind whistled and the small vessel threatened to founder at any moment. Maria Clara's voice had fallen silent. She was beside her man at the tiller.

The sea was sloshing the boat. The wind was trying hard to tear the sails. Only the glow of Master Manuel's pipe stood out, along with the figure of Quincas as he stood surrounded by the storm, impassive and majestic, the Old Sailor. The skiff was nearing the calm waters of the breakwater slowly and with difficulty. Just a little more and the festivities could begin again.

It was then that five flashes of lightning came, one after the other. The thunderclap echoed as if it were the end of the world. A huge wave picked up the skiff. The men and women cried out, and fat Margô wailed, "Oh, save me, Holy Mother!"

Amidst the roaring of the enraged sea, as the skiff stood in great peril, they saw, in the light of the flashes, Quincas jump, and they heard his last words.

The skiff was finally cutting through the calm waters by the breakwater, but Quincas stayed behind in the storm, wrapped in a sheet of waves and foam, by his own free will.

12

There was no way the undertaking establishment would take back the coffin, not even at half price. They had to pay, but Vanda did get the leftover candles. The coffin sits today in Eduardo's storeroom, with hopes of being sold second-hand to some corpse. As for Quincas's last words, there are differing versions. But who could have heard them clearly in the midst of that storm? A marketplace minstrel's version goes like this:

> *In the midst of the great uproar,*
> *Quincas was heard to say:*
> *"I'm burying me like I said I would*
> *And just when I want it to be.*
> *Let them keep their old coffin*
> *For some better time.*
> *I won't let them shove me*
> *Into some shallow ditch in the ground."*
> *The rest of his prayer*
> *Can never be known.*

Rio, April 1959.

THE STORY OF PENGUIN CLASSICS

Before 1946 . . . "Classics" are mainly the domain of academics and students; readable editions for everyone else are almost unheard of. This all changes when a little-known classicist, E. V. Rieu, presents Penguin founder Allen Lane with the translation of Homer's *Odyssey* that he has been working on in his spare time.

1946 Penguin Classics debuts with *The Odyssey*, which promptly sells three million copies. Suddenly, classics are no longer for the privileged few.

1950s Rieu, now series editor, turns to professional writers for the best modern, readable translations, including Dorothy L. Sayers's *Inferno* and Robert Graves's unexpurgated *Twelve Caesars*.

1960s The Classics are given the distinctive black covers that have remained a constant throughout the life of the series. Rieu retires in 1964, hailing the Penguin Classics list as "the greatest educative force of the twentieth century."

1970s A new generation of translators swells the Penguin Classics ranks, introducing readers of English to classics of world literature from more than twenty languages. The list grows to encompass more history, philosophy, science, religion, and politics.

1980s The Penguin American Library launches with titles such as *Uncle Tom's Cabin* and joins forces with Penguin Classics to provide the most comprehensive library of world literature available from any paperback publisher.

1990s The launch of Penguin Audiobooks brings the classics to a listening audience for the first time, and in 1999 the worldwide launch of the Penguin Classics Web site extends their reach to the global online community.

The 21st Century Penguin Classics are completely redesigned for the first time in nearly twenty years. This world-famous series now consists of more than 1,300 titles, making the widest range of the best books ever written available to millions—and constantly redefining what makes a "classic."

The Odyssey continues . . .

The best books ever written

PENGUIN CLASSICS

SINCE 1946

Find out more at www.penguinclassics.com

CLICK ON A CLASSIC
www.penguinclassics.com

The world's greatest literature at your fingertips

Constantly updated information on more than a thousand titles,
from Icelandic sagas to ancient Indian epics, Russian drama to
Italian romance, American greats to African masterpieces

•

The latest news on recent additions to the list, updated
editions, and specially commissioned translations

•

Original essays by leading writers

•

A wealth of background material, including biographies
of every classic author from Aristotle to Zamyatin, plot
synopses, readers' and teachers' guides, useful Web links

•

Online desk and examination copy assistance for academics

•

Trivia quizzes, competitions, giveaways, news on
forthcoming screen adaptations